SHARK LENGTHS
FROM SMALLEST TO LARGEST

Lehua and Kai 5 feet

Soccer Shark 5 feet

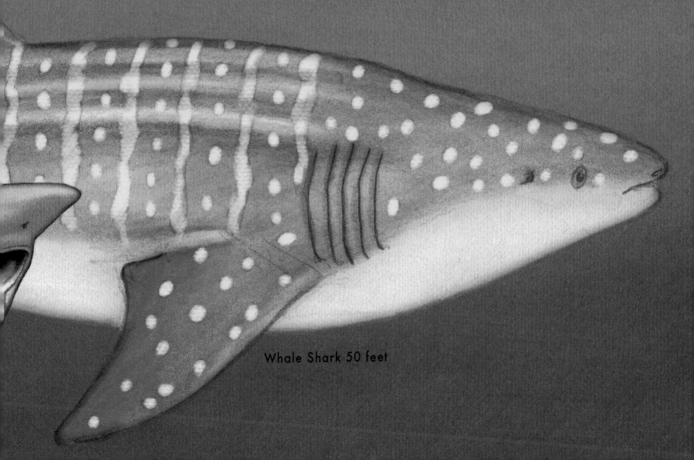

Whale Shark 50 feet

DEDICATION

Much Aloha to Elsa and Lauren.

— Ron Hirschi

To Cosmo and Bob, may you never lose your sense of wonder.

Love, Mom.

— Tammy Yee

ISBN: 978-1-949307-00-9
Library of Congress Control Number: 2019934482

First Printing, May 2019

Mutual Publishing, LLC
1215 Center Street, Suite 210
Honolulu, Hawai'i 96816
Ph: (808) 732-1709
Fax: (808) 734-4094
e-mail: info@mutualpublishing.com
www.mutualpublishing.com

Printed by RRD Shenzhen, China 02/2019

SHARK
Patrol

A DISCOVERY ADVENTURE IN HAWAI'I

written by **Ron Hirschi**

illustrated by **Tammy Yee**

Mutual Publishing

Shark Guy Kai

Aloha! Here we are in Hawai'i aboard the S.S. *Scoutabout.* We spent all last winter following humpback whales from Alaska to Hawai'i, and now we will spend the next year studying my favorite sea creatures—sharks! We set sail for California soon, but first we get to find out what we can about sharks here in warm island waters where they are known as manō.

Your Ocean Friend, Kai

Shark Guy Kai

Here's our crew:

Auntie Jan is a biologist.

Captain Mike is a fisherman who helps research projects like our shark studies.

My sister, Lehua, and I get to help in lots of ways, especially doing lots of sketching of the sharks we discover.

Our pup, Scout, keeps watch, perking her ears and wagging her tail when she hears singing whales…

I wonder if she'll be able to hear any sharks, but I don't think they sing. We'll find out!

KAI'S SHARK NOTES

Sharks swim the seas in many sizes and shapes. Some have razor sharp teeth. Others have hardly any teeth at all. Their sleek bodies and the shape of their scales help them slip quickly through the water. Their keen sense of smell, sharp eyesight, and pretty good hearing make them the best of predators.

Great white sharks and many others have large, sharp teeth, just right for catching fish and marine mammal prey. But the whale shark, the biggest shark and biggest fish of all, has tiny teeth almost hidden in its enormous mouth. A whale shark doesn't need big, sharp teeth since it isn't a predator. It feeds on plankton and tiny fish it scoops up while swimming through the sea with mouth open wide.

Great White Shark

Whale Shark

Tiger Shark

Whitetip Reef Shark

Lehua's Journal

Fisher Girl Lehua

I spend lots of my time fishing with friends, but I hope I never hook a great white or whale shark. They are soooo big, they would break my line for sure! 😱

Fisher Girl Lehua

Dear Shark Friends,

We snorkel every morning when we're in Hawai'i. It's so fun to see all the butterflyfish, parrotfish, and the little humuhumu, Hawai'i's state fish. Sometimes we see white tip reef sharks. They're about as long as I am tall and mostly friendly. But they do have sharp teeth and can be dangerous so we don't swim near them. Some people actually dive down and feed them. Not too smart!

Swimming with Humuhumu, Lehua

FROM THE DESK OF BIOLOGIST JAN

Some sharks live close to shore. Others live only at great depths or far out at sea.

White tip reef sharks are one of the most common sharks seen very close to Hawaiian shores. They usually spend the day tucked into a reef crevice or cave they return to time and time again. White tips grow to about five feet and prey on many kinds of reef fish, lobsters, and crab.

Ocean Guy Kai

Lehua and I went fishing from shore today. She caught some tasty ʻāweoweo for dinner. I caught a baby hammerhead shark! People think their head is shaped like a hammer, but I say it looks like my mountain bike's handlebars.

Fisher Girl Lehua

Auntie Jan helped Kai release this little hammerhead after we checked out its rough scales and weird head. She says their nostrils are set far apart just like their eyes. This helps them track down prey, picking up odors from one side then the other. Powerful receptors on the underside of their head make them even better predators. They swim close to the bottom and detect electro signals given off when rays, octopuses, and other creatures move their muscles. Even prey buried in the sand can be scooped for a meal, thanks to their special receptors.

FROM THE DESK OF BIOLOGIST JAN

Hammerhead sharks swim in from their open ocean homes to give birth in shallow waters. Like most sharks, their babies develop inside their mother's body and are born fully formed. Two feet at birth, young hammerheads swim to deeper waters as they grow, eventually reaching about 20 feet in length.

Fisher Girl Lehua

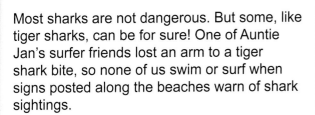

Most sharks are not dangerous. But some, like tiger sharks, can be for sure! One of Auntie Jan's surfer friends lost an arm to a tiger shark bite, so none of us swim or surf when signs posted along the beaches warn of shark sightings.

Lucky for us, we have a safe way to watch sharks of all kinds, thanks to Captain Mike's "Shark Cam." It's fun and cool with video game controls. Yesterday, we slipped it over a reef ledge and just as a huge school of fish swirled away, a huge tiger shark charged, maybe thinking the fish-shaped Shark Cam was an easy meal. As soon as we flashed the cam light, the tiger spooked and swam away, Shark Cam on its tail.

Captain Mike

Tiger sharks are well named, with their bold stripes and predatory ways. Prey includes many kinds of fish, lobsters, seals, sea turtles, and dolphins. They grow to eighteen feet and might weigh as much as two thousand pounds—a ton of tiger in the sea!

Tiger sharks live in tropical waters around the world. In Hawai'i, most shark attacks are the work of the tigers although others, including hammerheads, also pose a serious threat to swimmers and surfers.

Great white sharks might also attack people, but they usually live farther from shore than tiger sharks. Their pointy snout and white bellies help to identify these powerful predators.

Fisher Girl Lehua

Today we set sail for California in search of more kinds of sharks. We hardly got underway when Captain Mike made a quick stop to check out a herd of pilot whales. Auntie Jan says sharks like to hang out with these whales, so we dropped the Shark Cam overboard and scooted it around a bit.

Sure enough, there were beautiful oceanic whitetips cruising just below the surface. Their big, rounded dorsal fins are like soft mountains tipped in snow. Auntie Jan says their long pectoral fins help them to swim fast and far to catch fish as they cover miles of open ocean waters. 😊

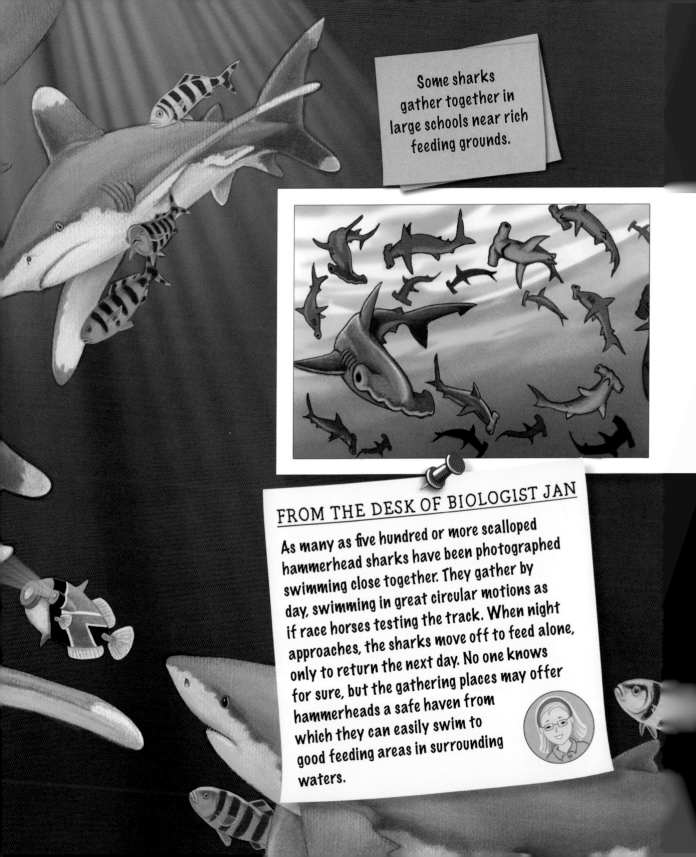

Some sharks gather together in large schools near rich feeding grounds.

FROM THE DESK OF BIOLOGIST JAN

As many as five hundred or more scalloped hammerhead sharks have been photographed swimming close together. They gather by day, swimming in great circular motions as if race horses testing the track. When night approaches, the sharks move off to feed alone, only to return the next day. No one knows for sure, but the gathering places may offer hammerheads a safe haven from which they can easily swim to good feeding areas in surrounding waters.

FROM THE DESK OF BIOLOGIST JAN

Others gather in schools during long distance migrations, much like humpback whales. Black tip sharks probably hold the record for the largest number of individuals traveling together. As many as 12,000 black tips will swim together as they migrate from the north Atlantic to summer breeding grounds in the Gulf of Mexico.

Shark Guy Kai

Shark Alert! **!!**

Captain Mike got a text today from Florida. A fisherman friend told him that a black tip shark attacked a man who was wading in shallow water. Captain Mike says these Atlantic sharks swim in huge schools, hugging the shore where they sometimes mistake a person for a meal when the water is murky from big winds and waves.

We're far from shore in clear Pacific waters, so we won't be troubled by black tips when we jump off the *Scoutabout* for a quick swim. But we hope to see other sharks soon, hopefully, the biggest of all, whale sharks.

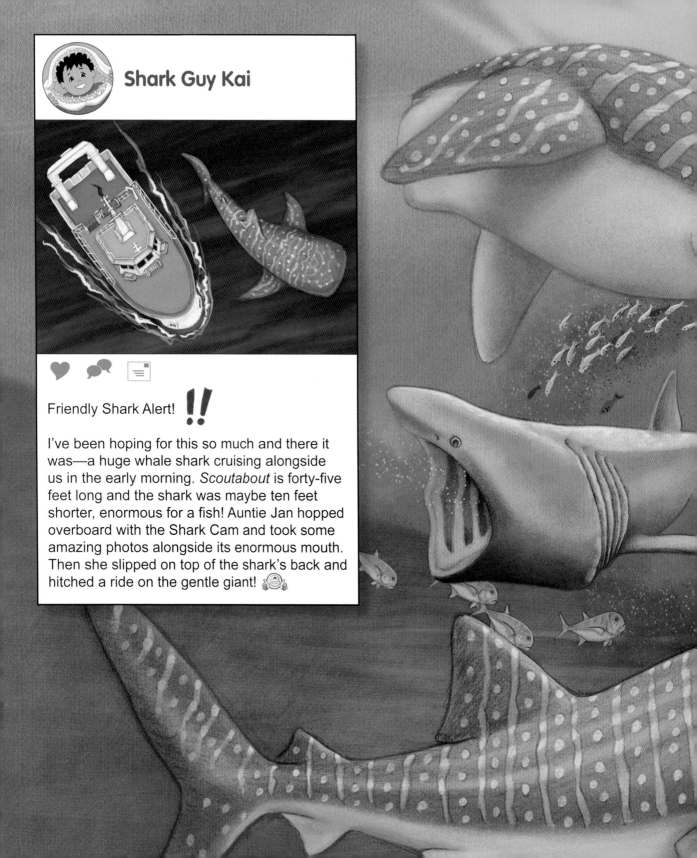

Shark Guy Kai

Friendly Shark Alert! **!!**

I've been hoping for this so much and there it was—a huge whale shark cruising alongside us in the early morning. *Scoutabout* is forty-five feet long and the shark was maybe ten feet shorter, enormous for a fish! Auntie Jan hopped overboard with the Shark Cam and took some amazing photos alongside its enormous mouth. Then she slipped on top of the shark's back and hitched a ride on the gentle giant!

KAI'S SHARK NOTES

Some sharks are mostly loners, cruising the ocean as they scoop plankton and tiny fish.

Whale sharks and basking sharks are two plankton feeders seen near the surface. Megamouth sharks also feed on plankton or other small sea creatures, but they live at great depths where no one has ever seen them in their natural habitat.

plankton

FROM THE DESK OF BIOLOGIST JAN

Whale sharks filter water through fine mesh strainers that trap plankton inside their huge mouths. In just one hour more than 160,000 gallons of water is filtered, supplying food for the giant sharks. But the strainers are so fine, they also trap oil and other pollutants that researchers worry may be killing whale sharks.

Shark Guy Kai

Here we are far from land but making headway to California.

Nighttime is amazing with no city lights, but with lights sparkling in the sea. Glowing jellyfish swarm by the millions and we know deeper down are some of the lesser known sharks. The Shark Cam can't dive deep enough to see them, but the smallest of all—the lantern shark—swims in the depths by day. Chemical reactions cause tiny dots on their belly to light up when lantern sharks swim up at night to feed close to the surface. I might have seen one last night, or maybe just in my shark dreams?

FROM THE DESK OF BIOLOGIST JAN

Not all that long ago, the very first megamouth shark was discovered in deep Hawaiian waters. Scientists know of other deep water sharks that swim up at night to feed on fish and squid. No doubt, many more sharks will be discovered since only 5% of the ocean has been studied. We can only guess what will be found in the 95% of ocean never studied or seen by human eyes—or Shark Cams!

KAI'S SHARK NOTES

Last night the Scoutabout rocked me gently in very calm waters while I dreamed about sharks. Well, they weren't real ones, but sharks I got to play soccer with, back home in the islands. We were chasing the ball together and all of a sudden one of the sharks slapped it with its tail. Goal!

Fisher Girl Lehua

We fished today as we got closer to the California coast. All of a sudden, Scout started barking when she finally heard sharks making some noise. We've figured out they don't sing like whales, but there was a whole lot of thrashing and splashing. It could only mean one thing—thresher sharks were fishing in their special way. We reeled in to watch their tails swirl and splash, not wanting to hook a thresher. Captain Mike says he used to catch them by accident when he tuna fished in Hawai'i.

Thresher sharks are easy to identify with their super long tail fin that can be half their body length or ten feet. They use their long tail to smack small fish, stunning their prey before turning quickly to snatch and swallow their meal. Threshers are not a threat to humans, although one person was hurt when he carelessly grabbed the tip of a thresher's tail.

10 feet

Fisher Girl Lehua
We all got up early this morning to see the coast of California for the first time. Better yet, as Auntie Jan had promised, really close to the boat, we saw a super high blow from a whale with a back that went on and on and on.

Fisher Girl Lehua
A blue whale! The largest creatures to have ever lived on earth, blue whales are coming back in good numbers just like humpbacks. Before the morning was over, we saw three of these amazing giants.

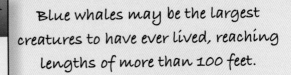

Blue whales may be the largest creatures to have ever lived, reaching lengths of more than 100 feet.

CHOMP! CHOMP!

But, they are pestered by one of the smallest shark one with very sharp teeth.

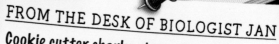

FROM THE DESK OF BIOLOGIST JAN

Cookie cutter sharks rise up from deep water and attach to blue whales and other marine mammals using their round mouth fitted with razor sharp teeth. Like a cutter you might use for sugar cookies, the little sharks bite deep and twist off a chunk of whale for a meal. No real harm done to the whale, the cookie cutter then dives deep until ready to feast again.

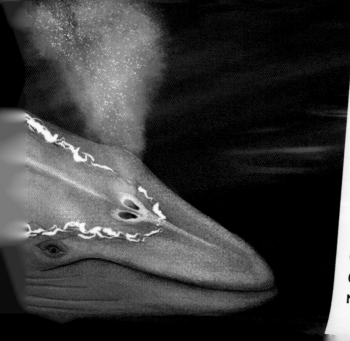

Shark Guy Kai

Fisher Girl Lehua

Auntie Jan heard from friends that hundreds, maybe thousands, of leopard sharks are dying in nearby San Francisco Bay. We sailed past San Francisco into Monterey Bay this morning while watching lots of leopard sharks on the Shark Cam. They looked so beautiful and healthy as they swam near sea otters in forests of iridescent kelp. News is that San Francisco Bay sharks are probably dying from all the pollution that enters the water there. Sea life in Monterey is doing better without big city pollution. We plan on finding ways of helping the water be cleaner!

We tied to a dock in Monterey Bay this morning after sailing nearby shores. We added a very cool horn shark to our list of shark species and watched lots of dolphins leaping offshore. Then, we had a fun day visiting the aquarium here that is so famous for doing such great shark research. Auntie Jan introduced us to lots of her friends from college days and they all gave us ideas of how to help sharks, like riding our bikes or taking the bus!

Friends of the Sea

Shark Explorers,

We saw lots of sharks on our journey, but we know there are way more than 400 different kinds of shark in the world ocean. So, our plan is to return to Hawai'i then on to the South Pacific and up to Japan to search for more sharks and other sea life. The two of us hope to see ALL the sharks around the globe and become the best ocean scientists we can be!

Aloha, Kai and Lehua

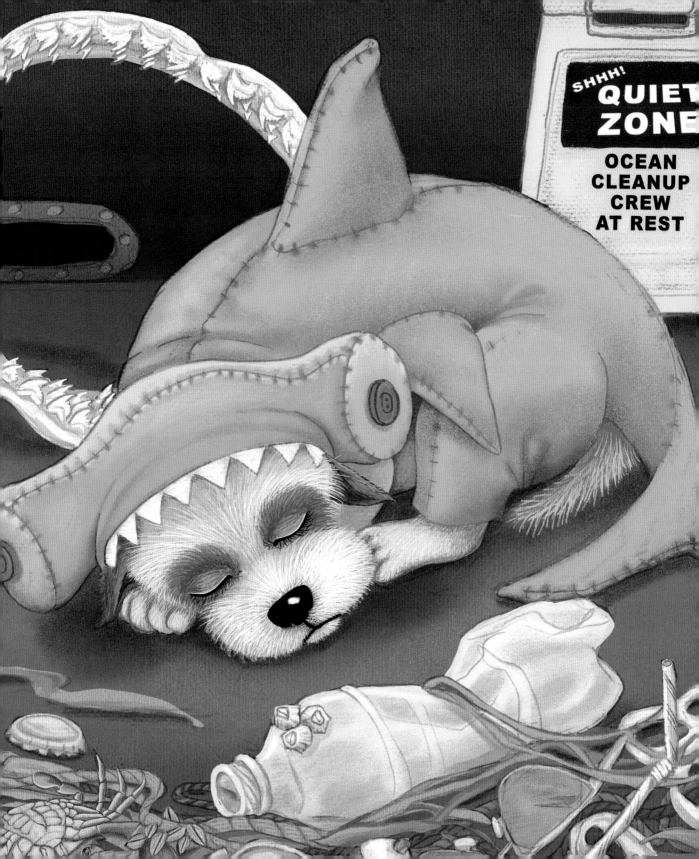

AFTERWORD

A lot of the pollution killing sharks and other fish of the Pacific and Atlantic Oceans comes from storm water runoff. This is mostly rainwater swishing and swirling along country roads, freeways, and city streets. The water flows into collection pipes and washes, untreated, into the ocean. The storm water carries with it oil and other fluids from cars, trucks, and other vehicles.

Kai and Lehua plan to do their part by walking, riding their bikes, and taking the bus whenever they can. By reducing rides in cars, they will help reduce the toxic pollution flowing into the sea. Since more than 500,000 cars, trucks and other vehicles are traveling on San Francisco streets, it is wise to find other ways to get around town. Seattle is also facing serious ocean pollution from its more than 500,000 vehicles. Salmon are dying from storm water pollution and little is known about affects on sharks. In Kai and Lehua's home state of Hawai'i more than one million cars add pollution to ocean waters where coral reefs, fish, and other creatures suffer from the toxin runoff. Thanks to Kai and Lehua for helping by doing small things that can make big changes for the ocean world.

ABOUT THE AUTHOR

Ron Hirschi grew up at the edge of an inland sea in Washington State. His dad built boats and Hirschi always had one to row or motor to his favorite fishing places. He spent many days fishing for salmon and sea going trout, but he and his buddy, Rick, also loved nothing better than to search for deep water where they fished endlessly for sharks. They kept other fish for family dinners, but always admired, then released the prized sharks.

Hirschi's love of fish and fishing led him to the University of Washington and a degree in fish and wildlife ecology. He has worked as a fish biologist, but has spent far more time writing nature books for young readers and taking kids out to rivers, streams, and the ocean to help them discover the fascinating world of fish and other aquatic creatures.

ABOUT THE ILLUSTRATOR

Tammy Yee grew up in Honolulu, Hawai'i, where she explored tide pools, swam in streams, and wrote and illustrated spooky stories her teachers politely read. After she graduated from college, she worked as a pediatric nurse. Having children rekindled her love for picture books, so in 1994 she exchanged her stethoscope for a paintbrush and has been illustrating ever since. Tammy has worked on more than thirty-six books, often with the help of her studio assistant, a burping bulldog named Roxy.

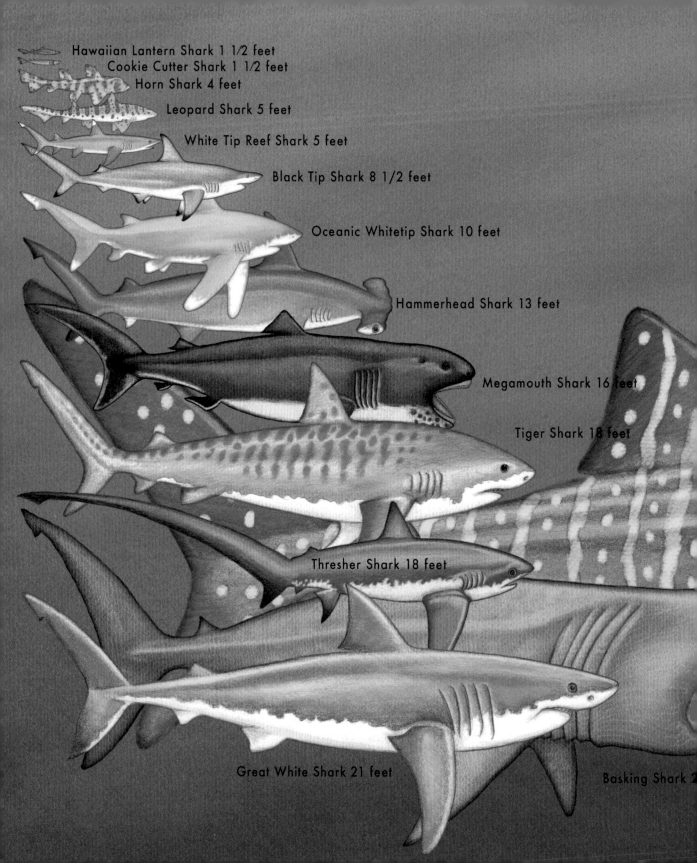

Hawaiian Lantern Shark 1 1/2 feet
Cookie Cutter Shark 1 1/2 feet
Horn Shark 4 feet
Leopard Shark 5 feet
White Tip Reef Shark 5 feet
Black Tip Shark 8 1/2 feet
Oceanic Whitetip Shark 10 feet
Hammerhead Shark 13 feet
Megamouth Shark 16 feet
Tiger Shark 18 feet
Thresher Shark 18 feet
Great White Shark 21 feet
Basking Shark